8/

The Case of the
Hat Burglar

Read more Jigsaw Jones Mysteries by James Preller

A JIGSAW JONES MYSTERY

The Case of the Hat Burglar

by James Preller
illustrated by R. W. Alley

FEIWEL AND FRIENDS
New York

A FEIWEL AND FRIENDS BOOK
An imprint of Macmillan Publishing Group, LLC
120 Broadway, New York, NY 10271

Our books may be purchased in bulk for promotional, educational, or business
use. Please contact your local bookseller or the Macmillan Corporate and
Premium Sales Department at (800) 221-7945 ext. 5442 or by email at
MacmillanSpecialMarkets@macmillan.com.

Library of Congress Cataloging-in-Publication Data

Names: Preller, James, author. | Alley, R. W., 1955- illustrator.
Title: The case of the hat burglar / by James Preller ; illustrated by R. W. Alley.
Description: New York : Feiwel and Friends, 2019. | Series: A Jigsaw Jones
mystery | Summary: First edition. | Summary: «Jigsaw Jones must solve find
the identity of the classroom thief, before they strike again"– Provided
by publisher.
Identifiers: LCCN 2018039222| ISBN 9781250207524 (hardcover) |
ISBN 9781250207531 (ebook) | ISBN 9781250207685 (pbk.)
Subjects: | CYAC: Mystery and detective stories. | Schools–Fiction. |
Stealing–Fiction.
Classification: LCC PZ7.P915 Carqp 2019 | DDC [Fic]–dc23
LC record available at https://lccn.loc.gov/2018039222

Book design by Véronique Lefèvre Sweet

Feiwel and Friends logo designed by Filomena Tuosto

First edition, 2019

mackids.com

In memory of Chris Porter—JP

CONTENTS

Chapter 1

Our Toughest Case

It reads "Theodore Jones" on my birth certificate. But, please, do me a favor. Don't call me that. My real name is Jigsaw.

Jigsaw Jones.

The way I see it, people should be able to make up their own names. After all, we're the ones who are stuck with them all our lives. Right? I get it. Our parents had to call us something when we were little—like "Biff" or "Rocko" or "Hey You!" But by age six, we should be allowed to name ourselves.

So I did. I took Jigsaw and tossed "Theodore" into the dumpster. These days, only two people call me Theodore. My mother, when she's unhappy. And my classmate Bobby Solofsky, when he wants to be annoying. Which is pretty much all the time. Bobby is a pain in my neck. Let me put it this way. Have you ever stepped on a Lego with your bare feet? There you are, cozy and sleepy, shuffling down the hallway in your pajamas, when suddenly—YOWZA!—you feel a stabbing pain in your foot.

What happened?

The Lego happened, that's what.

In my world, that Lego is named Bobby Solofsky.

And I'm the foot that stepped on it.

So, please, call me Jigsaw. After all, it's the name on the card.

NEED A MYSTERY SOLVED?

Call **Jigsaw Jones**
or **Mila Yeh**,
Private Eyes!

Mila is my partner and my best friend on the planet. I trust her 100 percent. Together, we make a pretty good team. We solve mysteries: lost bicycles, creepy scarecrows, surprise visitors from outer space, you name it. Put a dollar in our pockets, and we'll solve the case. Sometimes we do it for free.

But the Hat Burglar had us stumped.

We were baffled, bewildered, and bamboozled. There was a thief in our school, and I couldn't catch him. Or her. Because you never know about thieves. It could be anybody—he, she, or even it. That's true. *It happens*. We once caught a ferret red-handed. Or red-footed. Or red-pawed. Whatever! Point is, the ferret did it. But in this case, no matter what Mila and I tried, nothing worked. The mystery stayed a mystery. It was our toughest case yet. And by the end, the solution very nearly broke my heart.

But let me back up a bit. It all began last week, on a frosty Tuesday afternoon . . .

Chapter 2

Frozen

It was the coldest day of the year. Three degrees below zero. In other words, it felt like the planet Hoth from *Star Wars*. Or Canada, maybe. Even worse, there wasn't a single snowflake on the ground. Just cold wind and frozen skies. It was so nasty my dog, Rags, didn't want to go outside. And Rags *lives* for going outside. That morning, he stood by the open door, cold wind blasting his nose, and whined. "Sorry, Rags," my father insisted. "I don't like it any more than you do. But we gotta go."

Rags put on the brakes.

Eventually, my father talked Rags into it. I think he promised a treat. Looking outside, I felt the same way. I didn't want to leave my toasty house, either. But when my mother said, "Time for the bus, Jigsaw, no dillydallying," I had no choice.

My mother lets me dilly. And she lets me dally. But I can never dillydally. That's going too far. Not when there's a bus to catch.

At the bus stop, several kids stood together like a bunch of Popsicles in a freezer. I knew that two of them were Mila and Joey Pignattano, but it was hard to tell who was

who. Almost everyone was bundled in thick winter clothes, hats pulled down to their eyeballs. "Murfle, murfle," somebody mumbled to me through a wool scarf. I murfled back.

The wind snarled as if it were a snaggletoothed wolf.

Once the bus dropped us at school, we headed for our classrooms. Geetha Nair walked into room 201, dressed in a long colorful scarf wrapped around (and around!) her neck and face. The only part of her head that showed through were two round, chocolate-brown eyes.

Helen Zuckerman burst through the door. "I can't feel my nose," she announced. "It's frozen solid. I could snap it off like an icicle."

Joey poked Helen's nose with a finger. "Yipes, you're right, Helen. It's colder than ice cream."

Bigs Maloney, in contrast, strolled in wearing shorts and a long-sleeve shirt. "No coat, Bigs?" Ms. Gleason asked.

"It's in my backpack," he explained. "Just in case."

"Bigs, it's below zero outside. When are you going to put on a pair of long pants?" Helen wondered.

The big lug shrugged. "I like shorts better. They let my knees breathe."

"I wish it would snow," curly haired Lucy Hiller muttered. "I don't mind the cold if there's snow. Then we could go sledding . . . or build snow forts . . . or—"

"Make snow pies!" Joey cried.

"What?" Mila swung her backpack around with one hand. It landed softly at the bottom of her cubby. "Seriously, Joey. Snow pies?"

"Yes," Joey replied. "Snow pies are delicious. Only one ingredient: fresh, white, delicious snow. Yum!"

Stringbean Noonan gasped and pointed at Mila's hands. "Look, it's so cold your fingers turned purple!"

Mila laughed. She wiggled her fingers. "It's only nail polish, Stringbean. I had them done at the mall with Geetha and my stepmom this weekend."

"Phew!" said Stringbean. He seemed relieved.

Athena Lorenzo staggered into the room. "My hair. It was wet when I left my house. Now it's frozen solid!"

"Oh, Athena. Don't you have a hat?" Ms. Gleason asked.

"I used to," Athena said. "I think I lost it in school yesterday."

"Well, that's a problem," Ms. Gleason said. "Hats keep heads warm. It's important protection in this weather. Athena, do you know where we keep our Lost and Found?"

Athena shrugged. "I guess I lost that, too."

Ms. Gleason looked at me. I gave her a nod to let her know that I knew. "Jigsaw, could you please accompany Athena to the Lost and Found?"

"I can do it!" Bobby Solofsky volunteered. He pushed to the front of the room. "Let me take her, Ms. Gleason."

"Oh, that's very kind of you, Bobby," Ms. Gleason replied. "I'll think of you next time. For now, Jigsaw and Athena should get moving."

She turned to us. "Skedaddle, you two. Good luck finding your hat, Athena!"

"But!" Bobby protested.

"Next time, Bobby," Ms. Gleason said. There was ice water in her voice.

Chapter
3

Lost and Found . . . and Stolen?

Instead of calling it the "Lost and Found," they really should have named it "The Big Blue Bin." Because that's basically what it was. A big blue bin crammed with stuff. There was a long table beside it, also piled with gloves, scarves, books, coats, shoes, backpacks, and more.

Athena kneeled on the floor and began to dig through the messy blue bin.

"Anything?" I asked.

She shook her head.

I scanned the contents of the table. Holy wow. Kids sure lost a lot of stuff. Water bottles, books, and sneakers. And lots of winter clothes. Mittens, gloves, and scarves were everywhere.

But not a single hat.

Hmmmm, I wondered.

"Hey, Athena," I said. "Did you come across any hats in there?"

Athena shrugged. "I'm only looking for *my* hat. It's banana-colored. But now that you mention it, no, I don't see *any* hats in here."

"Maybe they keep hats in a special place," I suggested. "I'll check with Mrs. Garcia in the main office. She knows everything."

I found Mrs. Garcia at her desk. Behind her, a door led to the principal's office. Mrs. Garcia signaled for me to wait while she listened on a phone. Finally, she looked up and smiled. "Good morning, Mr. Jones. How can I help you?"

I told her about Athena's lost hat.

"Have you checked the Lost and Found?" she asked.

"Of course," I said. "But there are no hats."

"No hats? That can't be right. We find a lost hat practically every day." She rose and hustled out the door. I watched as she sorted through the items in the big blue bin.

"I'm sure we had at least a dozen hats here yesterday," Mrs. Garcia said. "I've been meaning to organize this mess, but there are only so many hours in the day."

"Are you the boss of it?" I asked.

Mrs. Garcia rubbed her forehead. She seemed stressed. It was a look I'd seen on my parents. A buzzer sounded from inside the office. Two grown-ups entered through the front doors, seeking help. Mrs. Garcia shook her head. "I do the best I can," she admitted. "But—"

"Too much to do, and not enough time to do it," I said.

"Exactly, Jigsaw," she agreed. "I don't know what to say about the missing hats. It's a mystery to me."

I reached into my pocket and handed her my card. "Mila and I might be able to help. For a dollar a day, we make problems go away."

Mrs. Garcia raised an eyebrow.

A second phone began to ring in the office.

"But this one's on me," I offered. "I can see you're busy. Mila and I will take this case for free."

"Do you really think it's necessary?" Mrs. Garcia asked.

I nodded grimly. "It looks to me like we've got a hat burglar. You'll need a detective to get to the bottom of it. Otherwise, we'll have a lot of cold heads around here."

Mrs. Garcia reached out a hand. We shook on it. "Deal," she said.

Chapter 4

On the Case

Like always, I sat across from Mila in the lunchroom. But instead of eating my soggy tuna-fish sandwich, I opened my detective journal to a clean page. I wrote:

THE CASE OF THE HAT BURGLAR
CLIENT: Mrs. Garcia
SUSPECTS: Bobby Solofsky,
Athena Lorenzo

Mila pointed to my list of suspects. "Why them?"

"We have to start somewhere. This list will get longer before we're finished." I continued, "Athena said she didn't know where the Lost and Found was. I thought it was suspicious."

"You didn't believe her?" Mila asked.

I shrugged. "How do you not know?"

"People are funny," Mila said. "They don't know all sorts of things. And that goes double for Athena."

"Of course, I *always* suspect Solofsky," I explained. "When you hear hoofbeats, think horses, not zebras."

"Excuse me?"

"It's something my father says," I told her. "It means that you should start with the obvious answer, not some wild explanation."

"Oh," Mila said, thinking it over. "So if you hear hooves . . . it's probably not a rhinoceros."

"Not around here, anyway," I said, laughing. "I'm going to pay a surprise visit to Solofsky this afternoon."

"Good thinking," Mila said. "I'd join you, but I have to stay after school today. I've got this piano thing."

"A piano thing?" I repeated. "It's a thing now?"

"A lesson, okay," Mila replied. "I've got a recital coming up. But while I'm here, I can snoop around. Maybe I can locate witnesses."

"Sounds like a plan," I said.

"Good, so what's next?" Mila asked.

I eyeballed my soggy tuna-fish sandwich. "The saddest sandwich ever," I groaned.

"Here, try this instead," Mila offered. She slid half of her peanut-butter-and-jelly sandwich in my direction.

"Really? Thanks, Mila—you're the best."

"No worries," Mila replied.

I wrote the word *MOTIVE* in my journal using capital letters. I scribbled in three question marks. "One thing bugs me, Mila. Why would someone take all the hats?"

Mila looked out the window, as if the answer might be floating outside somewhere, like a lonely cloud. She finally raised two hands and said, "I don't know. Maybe the thief has a thing for hats?"

I snorted. "Too weird."

"Maybe it's about the Lost and Found," Mila suggested. "Maybe someone is trying to teach kids a lesson about not picking up their stuff?"

"Maybe," I murmured. "But who? Mrs. Garcia? I got the impression she thought running the Lost and Found was a big headache."

"She's very busy," Mila noted. "Maybe it would be easier for her if, I don't know, there were fewer hats? Anyway, better add Mrs. Garcia to the list."

I wasn't sure, but I followed Mila's suggestion. One thing I know about Mila—she's usually right.

Chapter 5

Solofsky Clowns Around

That afternoon, I walked up the stone path to Bobby Solofsky's front door. A strong wind tried to knock me off my feet. I hoped Bobby was home. I didn't think I could take another five minutes out in this snarling cold.

I pushed the doorbell.

Nothing happened.

I pushed again.

Nothing happened all over again.

As I turned to leave, the door slowly squeaked open.

No one was there.

Strange.

"Hello?" I called out.

Silence.

I took a cautious step forward.

"YAH!" a loud voice screamed. Bobby leaped out from behind the door, arms raised high. He was wearing a clown mask.

I nearly jumped out of my socks.

"BWA-HA-HA-HA!" Bobby cried, doubling over in laughter. He removed the mask. "Scared you, didn't I?"

"Stop clowning around," I muttered. "Let me inside, Bobby. You nearly gave me a heart attack."

Once I was inside, Bobby slammed the door shut. "Just dump your stuff on that chair, Theodore."

I dumped it all—hat, shoes, gloves, scarf, sweater, and coat.

I looked around. "Is anybody home?"

"Nah," Bobby said. "My sister, Karla, is supposed to be watching me. But she went across the street to her friend's place. I'm used to it."

I thought about my own house. My dog, my sister, three brothers, Grams, and two parents. I was never home alone.

I shivered. "Do you know how to make hot chocolate? I feel like I have ice cubes for toes."

Bobby rattled around in the kitchen. He boiled water. He opened and shut cupboards. He zapped a bag of popcorn in the microwave. *Zing!* It was done. I was impressed. Bobby sure knew his way around the kitchen. He seemed used to taking care of himself.

I took a sip of hot chocolate. The temperature was perfect. "You don't happen to have any whipped cream, do you?" I asked.

Bobby made a face. "This isn't a restaurant, Jones. Why are you here, anyway? It's not like we're friends."

He caught me off guard. There was something different in his voice. Anger, I

guess, but also sadness. I decided to take the direct approach.

"Someone has been stealing hats from the school's Lost and Found," I said. "I wondered if you knew anything about it."

I watched him closely. Any good detective knows that liars often give themselves away. Lying makes most people uncomfortable.

Before telling a lie, they might blink frequently, or look away, or nervously tug on an earlobe. I studied Solofsky for any telltale signs.

Instead, Bobby slid his tongue across his teeth. He made a sucking sound. Normal for Solofsky. He did that all the time. Bobby had the manners of an orangutan. He scoffed,

"What would I do with a bunch of dumb hats?"

Bobby didn't deny doing it. He didn't bother.

And at that moment, I knew he was innocent.

"Sure, I believe you, Solofsky," I said. "But let me ask you one more thing."

"One thing," he said, crossing his arms. "Then it's time for you to scram. I don't like being treated like a cheap crook. Hats! Come on. That's not my style."

"I'm sorry if I insulted you," I said. "I'm trying to help the kids in our school. There's going to be a lot of frozen ears if I can't crack this case."

Bobby shoved a fistful of popcorn into his mouth. He didn't seem to care one way or another.

"You're a smart guy, Solofsky. Why do *you* think someone would steal hats?" I asked.

Bobby leaned back in his chair. He let out a soft burp. "Money," he said. "Money makes the world go round. Maybe the burglar hopes to sell them. Make some easy cash."

"Maybe," I said.

But I doubted it.

After all, who buys used hats?

The crime didn't make sense. Where was the motive?

I thanked him and stood to leave.

Bobby watched me walk away from the doorway of a big, empty house.

He seemed almost sad to see me go.

I learned two things from my visit. I realized that Bobby Solofsky was a lonely kid in a big, empty house. And I knew in my bones that Bobby didn't steal the hats.

Chapter 6

The Burglar Strikes Again!

Mrs. Garcia found us when the front doors of the school opened in the morning. "Jigsaw, Mila! I'm glad you're here." She took off her glasses and waved them in her hand. "We've been hit again!"

"What, more hats?" I asked.

"No, this is worse. Much worse." She gestured for us to follow her. It didn't take a rocket scientist to know where we were going. She stopped at the big blue bin. Yesterday, it was overflowing. Today, it was only halfway full. I studied the table. There were still a bunch of items there—water bottles and lunch boxes and binders—but it wasn't as cluttered as yesterday.

"Look at this!" Mrs. Garcia exclaimed. She seemed genuinely upset. "All the gloves and mittens. Gone!"

"It's true, Jigsaw," Mila said, after sorting through the bin. "Not a single glove or mitten. That's bizarre."

I scratched the back of my neck. First hats. Now gloves and mittens. What in the world was going on? "When did you first notice?" I asked Mrs. Garcia.

"I came in early to neaten up. It's always such a disaster area," Mrs. Garcia explained. "I knew something was wrong right away."

I looked at Mila. "You were here yesterday afternoon. Did you see anything?"

"I wish," Mila said. "Everything seemed normal. Then I had my lesson in the music room."

"Was anyone around?" I asked.

Mila shut her eyes, concentrating. "A couple of teachers. Mr. Copabianco, the custodian. Maybe some students. Plus, there's always School's Out."

"Mila's right," Mrs. Garcia noted. "There's usually about thirty, forty students who stay late for pickup. Their parents work, and so on."

"Are they free to wander around?" I asked.

Mrs. Garcia opened her palms. "I surely think not."

Mila pointed across the hall. There were two bathroom doors, labeled BOYS and GIRLS.

"Well, yes," Mrs. Garcia said. "They have access to the bathroom."

"Which is right across from the Lost and Found," Mila said. She turned to me. "This won't be easy, Jigsaw. There are dozens of kids in School's Out every afternoon."

I frowned. "Oh, great. That's terrific. Our list of suspects just got a whole lot longer. Every one of those kids had an opportunity to commit the crime."

On the way to class, Mila seemed downhearted. "I'm sorry, Jigsaw. I feel like I let you down."

"Don't be silly, Mila," I said. "You had your piano lesson. I was off questioning Solofsky. We can't be everywhere at once."

I stopped in my tracks. I tried to snap my fingers—*snap!*—but snapping fingers is not exactly one of my big talents. It sounded more like *fillupf*. Yeesh. I said, "I know who can help us!"

"Yeah, who?" Mila asked.

"Reginald Pinkerton Armitage the Third," I said. "He owes me a favor. In fact, Reggie owes me a bunch of favors!"

From that moment on, I felt as light as air. I finally had a plan to catch the Hat Burglar. I floated down the hall and into our classroom. Pretty good, especially since I carried a super-heavy backpack. All the kids do. *Thud*, *clunk*. I dropped the pack in my cubby. It was like lifting a piano off my back. I love books, but they sure are heavy.

Whew!

Now we just needed to get through the school day—and then pay a visit to the richest kid in town.

Chapter 7

Reginald's Gadgets and Gizmos

At the front curb, my brother Billy rolled down the driver's-side window. He called, "I'll be back to pick you up in an hour, Worm!"

"Thanks for the ride," I called back. "But don't call me Worm!"

He zoomed away, leaving Mila and me at Reginald's front door. I did a few push-ups on the doorbell. *Gong-gong-gong.*

Mila shivered. She blew clouds of cold air from her mouth.

"Reginald expects us," I said. "I told him all about the case."

The front door opened. "Jigsaw and Mila! Splendid, splendid!" Reginald ushered us inside. "It's frightfully cold out there."

"Yeah, frightfully," I echoed.

I noticed that Reginald had on a pair of baby blue bunny slippers. The slippers looked toasty, but they didn't match his outfit. He wore a sweater-vest over a white shirt and a yellow bow tie. Neat and tidy, as always.

I was glad I didn't have holes in the toes of my socks.

We shed our winter clothes and kicked off our shoes. Those were the house rules: no shoes, sneakers, or boots. Reginald handed our things to a tall butler, Gus, who had appeared at his side.

"May I take your hat?" Gus asked.

"No, thanks, Gus," I replied. "There's too much of that going around already."

He raised an eyebrow, confused.

"Hat burglars," I explained. "It's a thing

now. I'd prefer to keep this one on my head, if you don't mind. We're kind of a team."

Gus harrumphed and said, "Suit yourself."

I harrumphed back.

"Reggie, your house is amazing!" Mila gushed. And she was right. It was amazing—if you liked things like indoor swimming pools and private game rooms and seventeen glistening bathrooms with gold faucets.

I thought it was a little much.

We followed Reginald down a long hallway.

A while back, Reginald had started his own "secret agent" business. It didn't work out so well. He thought being a detective would be fun, a chance to play with fancy gadgets and gizmos. But Reginald learned that solving mysteries could be a rough

business. It took hard work and brainpower. Reggie was a nice kid, but he was as tough as a silk pillow. He promised I could borrow his gadgets anytime.

Today, I needed him to keep that promise.

Reginald pushed open a door, then said over his shoulder to Mila, "Please come into my research room."

I'd been here once before. The room looked like a laboratory. Various objects had been placed on marble countertops. "This is all your spy equipment?" Mila asked.

She picked up an old boot.

It was a mistake I'd once made myself. "Be careful, Mila," I warned.

Sploinnng! A suction cup attached to a spring popped out of the sole.

"Whoa," Mila said, jumping back in surprise.

"Suction-cup boots," Reginald explained. "For walking on ceilings."

"It really works?" Mila asked.

Reginald shrugged and admitted, "I'm afraid to find out."

Mila picked up two plastic goldfish. "What are these?"

"Underwater walkie-talkies," Reginald explained.

"Glub, glub," I commented—for no reason at all.

"And this?" Mila pointed to a tray of cucumber sandwiches. "Let me guess. Is it some kind of secret listening device?"

"No, it's a tray of cucumber sandwiches," Reginald said. "For snack time."

"Cucumber sandwiches, yum," I groaned. It was the last thing in the world I'd want to eat. I was a peanut-butter-and-jelly kind of guy. "Sadly, Reggie, we don't have time for snacks. We're here on business."

Reginald perked up when I told him we needed a way to keep an eye on the Lost and Found.

"We can't be there to watch it all the time," Mila explained.

"Ah, I have just the thing." Reginald walked across the room and picked up a guinea pig plush toy.

"A plush toy?" Mila said.

Reginald used a pinkie to push his glasses back up his nose. "It contains a motion-sensitive camera. The very latest technology," he said. "My father got it on one of his business trips. Just point the nose to the area you wish to watch, and the camera automatically snaps a photo whenever anyone walks past."

Mila examined it closely. "Perfect," she announced. "And cute, too."

"I can have the photos sent to you—to a cell phone, laptop, home computer, whatever you'd like," Reginald offered. He handed me a headset. "If you'd like, we can communicate using this. Stereo sound, naturally."

I shook his hand. "Reggie, you're the cat's meow."

He smiled broadly. "My pleasure, Jones. I'm happy to help. But before you go, please take a moment to enjoy a delicious cucumber and cream cheese sandwich."

He looked up at me through round, hopeful eyes.

I frowned at the tray of sandwiches.

Mila's eyes twinkled and she gave me a secret nod. I knew what I had to do.

"Sure," I said to my friend, Reginald Pinkerton Armitage the Third. "Who doesn't love a cucumber sandwich?"

Chapter 8

The Setup

On Thursday afternoon, Mila and I stood in the hallway outside the main office. Mrs. Garcia slid open the glass case. It was filled with trophies, art projects, photos, and other school memorabilia.

I handed her the guinea pig.

The school secretary placed it on the middle shelf.

"Make sure it faces the Lost and Found table," I instructed her.

Mrs. Garcia moved it slightly.

"What do you think, Mila?" I asked.

"Looks good," my partner said.

I slid the bin a few inches closer to the table. "Now when anyone stops by, the hidden camera will snap a series of photos. If the Hat Burglar strikes, we'll have the proof we need."

"I'm very impressed," Mrs. Garcia said. "You two do nice work."

"It's a living," I said.

Mrs. Garcia made a fist and punched the palm of her other hand. "We'll catch that burglar yet!" She clucked her tongue. "Tsk, tsk. Taking children's hats and mittens! What a terrible thing!"

"Just awful," Mila agreed.

"Oh, I almost forgot," I said. "This trap won't work unless the Hat Burglar returns to the scene of the crime. We need to sweeten the prize." I took the baseball hat off my head . . . and placed it on the table.

"Jigsaw! No way," Mila said. "You love that hat. You wear it all the time."

I shrugged. "It's okay, Mila. No burglar will be able to resist this hat."

Mila pulled on her long black hair. It was how she got her Thinking Machine working. She looked at the guinea pig, then back at the table.

"You okay?" I asked.

"Yeah." Mila nodded. "This will work just fine."

Chapter 9

The Clue

Five days slowly passed—Thursday, Friday, Saturday, Sunday, Monday—and nothing happened. But on Tuesday, the Hat Burglar struck again.

And this time, we were ready.

I stood at the Lost and Found, staring at a nearly empty blue bin. This time, the missing items were scarves and sweaters and snow pants. Pretty much anything that could be worn. All gone.

All except for my baseball hat.

Mila lifted it off the table, smiling. "Look, Jigsaw. Your hat. It's still here!"

I pulled it down over my head.

Snug as a bug in a rug.

I looked at the hidden camera. The guinea pig's beady little eyes stared directly at me. "I can't wait to get home to see what shows up in the pictures."

"Right," Mila said. "I'd love to be there, but I've got to practice my piece for the piano recital. It's a real knuckle buster."

"Too bad," I said. "You'll miss out on the fun."

The rest of the school day crawled by like a tortoise with a sprained ankle. Finally, the bell rang. Time to hurry home.

Within minutes, I was ready. I set up my laptop on our dining room table. Rags lay by my feet. I spoke into the headset microphone. "Reggie, this is Jigsaw."

"Roger that. The eagle has landed!" Reginald said.

"Excuse me?" I asked.

"I mean, what's up?" Reginald replied.

I explained that the crime occurred sometime between 3:20 on Monday afternoon, when school got out, and 9:20 on Tuesday morning. "Can I see all the photos that were taken in that time period?"

"Certainly."

I could hear the *tap-tap-tapping* of computer keys.

A file appeared on my screen. I double-clicked and scrolled through a series of images. Nothing much captured my attention. Ralphie Jordan came by and took a water bottle. He seemed happy. That made sense. It was a Lost and Found, after all. Geetha stopped by. She looked through the items but left without taking anything. It made me wonder what she was doing. I'd have to ask her about it later. I saw images of kids from School's Out. They went in and out of the bathroom. They drank at the water fountain. But not a single one stopped at the Lost and Found.

Then something took my breath away.

In a series of photos, I saw a hand reach up from below. Fingers grabbed the guinea pig and turned it until the camera faced the wall. The image went gray.

Nothing, zippo, zilch.

But then . . . the guinea pig swiveled back. The fingers had returned. The hidden camera once again faced the Lost and Found table. But now, items were missing. The Hat Burglar had beaten us again.

"Did you see that, Reggie?!" I exclaimed. "We've been outsmarted!"

"Indeed," he murmured.

"This burglar has been one step ahead of us the entire time. That's three robberies!" I groaned. "And we've got nothing!"

I wished Mila were with me. She always had good ideas when cases went bad. I missed my partner.

Reginald didn't speak. I could sense him in my headset, waiting. Finally, he asked, in a soft voice, "Jigsaw, I must ask. Besides Mila, who else knew about the guinea pig?"

I didn't answer.

I didn't want to say the words.

And I hoped with all my heart that I was wrong.

There had to be another explanation.

"Jigsaw?" he repeated. "Are you still there?"

"Hold on, let me think," I snapped.

"Of course," Reginald answered.

"Okay," I said. "Let's look at those last few photos again. The ones that showed the hand. Maybe there's a ring or some other clue."

I knew that Mrs. Garcia wore a diamond ring on her left hand. Reginald brought them up on the screen. The fingers were a fleshy blur. "Can you enhance the image?" I asked.

Reginald clicked keys. He hummed tunelessly while he worked. The photo came into sharper focus.

I stared at the picture.

My heart climbed up my throat.

"Larger, Reggie," I said, my voice scarcely a whisper. "Focus on the fingernails. I need to be sure."

The photograph got sharper, larger. There could be no doubt. Each nail was covered with polish.

Purple nail polish.

Chapter 10

Double-Crossed

I went into the kitchen and poured myself a tall glass of grape juice. I slugged it down. Then I had another. It didn't wash away the sour feeling in my stomach.

I tried doing a jigsaw puzzle in my bedroom.

Step-by-step, I put the pieces together.

I couldn't stop thinking about the case.

And about my best friend in the world.

The clues had been there all along. They piled up, one after another. I took notes in my detective journal. It helped to get my thoughts down on paper.

I had thought about *motive*, and I had thought about *opportunity*. But I had forgotten to think about *method*.

How did the Hat Burglar do it?

How does a thief walk away with all those hats and mittens? Wouldn't someone notice?

I remembered the morning when this case began. We were in Ms. Gleason's class. *Mila swung her backpack around with one hand.* It landed softly, *soundlessly*, at the bottom of her cubby.

How could that be possible?

Because it wasn't filled with books!

Mila wasn't much help on this case. She kept making excuses. She said she had piano lessons, a big recital. I wondered if any of that were true.

Another thing popped into my brain. Mila told Stringbean that she and Geetha had their nails done at the mall. *She wiggled her purple fingernails.*

Could it have been Geetha?

I closed my eyes to help me remember. No, Geetha's fingernails were bright red.

Could they have teamed up together?

Mila knew about the hidden camera. That must have spoiled her plans. For a while, anyway. Then she figured out a solution. She didn't realize that I'd still be able to catch her red-handed.

Or, in this case, purple-handed.

Sigh.

I looked down at the rug. My puzzle was finished. One hungry cat staring at three nervous goldfish in a bowl. I knew what I had to do next.

"Hello?"

"Hi, Mila," I spoke into the phone.

There was a pause. "Oh, hey, Jigsaw. What's up?"

I told her exactly what was up.

She listened in silence.

"Tell me I'm wrong," I pleaded. "Please, Mila. Tell me I've gotten this all mixed up."

She was so quiet I couldn't even hear her breathe. "I won't lie to you," she finally said.

That's when I told my ex–best friend that we couldn't be partners anymore. It was over. "You were my partner," I said. "I trusted you."

Mila didn't answer.

Or maybe I didn't listen.

Maybe I had already hung up the phone.

Five minutes later, Rags barked at the front door. We didn't need a doorbell as long as Rags was around. I rushed to get there first.

There Mila stood, staring at me with red-rimmed eyes. She had a scarf wrapped around her neck and mouth.

"I don't feel like talking," I said.

Mila nodded, as if she expected it. Instead, she reached out a hand. It held a piece of paper.

I moved to close the door.

Mila stuck out her foot.

"Take it!" she demanded.

I grabbed the paper and shoved it into my pocket.

"Okay," I said. "We're done now?"

Then I slowly, slowly closed the door as she stood there, unmoving. Her eyes never left my face.

Click. The door shut.

My mother called from the kitchen. "Who was that at the door, Jigsaw?"

"No one," I said. "Nobody at all."

I walked into my bedroom, took the paper out of my pocket, crumpled it into a ball, and tossed it into the wastebasket.

Face-to-Face

I tossed and turned, unable to sleep.

My mind kept returning to that crumpled-up scrap of paper at the bottom of my wastebasket.

I got up, banged my knee in the dark (ouch!), and fished it out. I switched on the desk lamp. I smoothed out the paper on the table.

It was in code, obviously. I scanned it up, down, and sideways. I waited to see if any words came to me. *Or, in, end, ever.* It didn't mean anything to me.

IAMSOS
OR
RYPL
EASELE
TMEEXPL
AINYO
URB
ESTF
RIENDFO
REVERM
ILA

Next, I wrote out all the letters again:

IAMSOSORRYPLEASELETME
EXPLAINYOURBESTFRIEND
FOREVERMILA

I let my mind go blank. I scanned the letters to see if more words popped out. And they did. In moments, the entire message became clear. Mila had written a simple Space Code. For a twist, she wrote it vertically. Clever girl.

She wanted me to understand.

I drew a slanted line where the spaces between the words were supposed to be.

I/AM/SO/SORRY/PLEASE/LET/ME/
EXPLAIN/YOUR/BEST/FRIEND/
FOREVER/MILA

I turned off the lamp and crawled back into bed.

It was a long time before I got to sleep.

The next morning, I saw Mila at the bus stop. It was still cold, but the sky was blue and the sun was out. She looked at me. I looked away.

"They say it might snow tonight," Mila said.

I didn't answer.

Her shoulders sagged.

When the bus came, Mila climbed on first. She passed our regular seats and, instead, took a seat in the last row. All by herself.

I followed, walking slowly.

"Slide over," I said.

Mila looked up. Her eyes flickered. She moved to give me room. "Jigsaw, I—"

I shook my head. "I read your note," I said. "A vertical Space Code. It didn't take long to figure out."

Mila nodded, waiting.

"You want me to forgive you," I said. "I don't know about that. But I will listen. We go back a long time. I owe you that much."

Mila leaned forward, her eyes locked on mine. Before she could speak, I raised two fingers. "I need to know two things, Mila. Why did you do it? And why didn't you tell me?"

Mila stammered, "I didn't—I mean, I don't—it's hard—"

"Just spill it," I said.

Mila tightened her lips. She nodded. "Okay, but promise you'll really listen."

I frowned and crossed my arms.

Mila looked out the window. Houses and trees sailed past like boats on a river. "Every day at school, I look at that Lost and Found," she began. "It's always filled with stuff. Beautiful jackets, warm hats, books, scarves—and it just sits there for weeks and weeks. So many kids never bother to look for their lost things." She paused. "It makes me mad, Jigsaw."

"Mad?" I said.

"Yes, angry," Mila said. There was fire in her eyes. She grabbed my arm. "A couple of weeks ago, at my church, they started talking about the homeless, and the poor. There are people who don't have anything, Jigsaw! It's bitterly cold outside." She gestured to everyone sitting on the bus. "And we have so much. It doesn't seem fair."

That's when I saw it. The wetness in her eyes, like stones in a riverbed. Her cheeks were flushed. Mila was upset.

"So you stole?" I said.

Mila hung her head. "I'll return everything," she said. "It's just . . . there are families that need help, Jigsaw. Children like us. I wanted to donate the clothes to charity."

"You could have told me," I said.

"No, I couldn't. Not the great Jigsaw Jones," Mila said. The whisper of a smile crossed her face. "You would have never gone along with it."

We both knew she was right.

"Fair enough," I said.

The tension eased between us.

My best friend bit her lip. She brushed a strand of hair from her face. "Really?" she said. "You're not mad?"

I sighed. "I'm not happy, Mila. But no one in this world is perfect. Not even you."

She sniffled and grinned.

I said, "You did the wrong thing, Mila—but for all the right reasons. You've got a good heart. You'll have to apologize to Mrs. Garcia. And you'll have to return all the lost items."

Mila nodded. "Yes, I know."

"I have to say, though. It was pretty smart," I admitted. "I suppose you used your backpack to carry the clothes."

Mila nodded. "And Geetha's cello case."

"I thought you might have had help," I said. "You never took my hat."

"No, I couldn't do that," Mila admitted.

"Maybe it was a clue," I reasoned. "Maybe, deep down, you wanted to get caught."

Mila slumped in her seat. "How can I fix this?"

I leaned back, kicked my legs out, and cradled my hands behind my head. "I think this might work out after all," I said. "Because I just had a pretty terrific idea."

Chapter 12

The Community Comes Out

It was Friday afternoon two weeks later. Still cold out, but now the world was white and sparkling with snow. Mila and I sat with Mrs. Garcia behind a table facing the front doors of the school. It was the deadline for all Lost and Found items. If any items were still left after today, the school would donate them to charity.

"It really is a lovely idea," Mrs. Garcia said. "You know, Mila, as a matter of fact, we do give away the items at the end of the school year. We've always done that since

I've worked here. But I think you're right. It's important to do it in the winter, too. This is a hard time of year for people in need."

Mila blushed. "Well, I'm just glad—I mean—you've been so nice about everything."

"Some of this was my fault," Mrs. Garcia said. "I was so busy, I dumped all the items in the blue bin. Very helter-skelter. It made it hard for kids to find their things."

"It looks amazing now," I said.

Bigs Maloney's father had volunteered to build a shelving unit for the Lost and Found. Coats and sweaters were now neatly displayed on wire hangers. There was a shelf for water bottles only. Another shelf for lost books. He even painted a fancy sign.

"I adore the clothesline idea," Mrs. Garcia gushed. Across the back wall, hats and gloves were attached to a rope with clothespins. "It's so much easier now."

A few students came by to pick up lost items. Poor Athena never did find her banana-colored hat. I was surprised when Bobby Solofsky showed up. He held the front door open for his mother, who was carrying a cardboard box. Mrs. Garcia looked up. "Hello, Mrs. Solofsky. Are you here to pick up items from the Lost and Found?"

"Not exactly," Mrs. Solofsky said. She plopped the heavy box on the ground. "We were hoping to donate more clothes."

"What?" Mrs. Garcia said.

"Bobby told me about the donation," Mrs. Solofsky said, smiling at Mila and me. "So we put our heads together. We thought, well, maybe we could do something to help. So Bobby and I cleaned out our closets and found all sorts of clothes that don't fit anymore."

Bobby stood next to his mother, beaming. It looked as if he'd grown two inches

overnight. Maybe there was still hope in the world. Maybe Solofsky was beginning to see the light. *It felt good to do good.*

In the next few minutes, more families showed up—carrying bags and boxes filled

with clothes. Soon we had lots more clothing to give. Because the people in our community wanted to make a difference.

Mila and I sorted through the donated items, piling them neatly. Bobby came over to lend a hand. I whispered to Mila, "You did this."

She shrugged and looked down. "I don't know. Seems like a lot of people helped."

"No, it was your idea," I said. "That's where it started. You're a good person, Mila Yeh. And I'm proud we're best friends."

"And partners?" Mila asked.

"Yes," I laughed. "And partners!"